MW00938271

Dragon Eggs Book 1

Dragon's Egg

Emily Martha Sorensen

Also by Emily Martha Sorensen

Books:

Black Magic Academy
The Keeper and the Rulership
The Fires of the Rulership

Fairy Senses:

Fairy Eyeglasses
Fairy Compass
Fairy Earmuffs
Fairy Barometer
Fairy Pox
Fairy Slippers

Short Story Collections:

Worlds of Wonder

Comics:

A Magical Roommate
(available in-print or online)

To Prevent World Peace
(available in-print or online)

Dragon Eggs Book #1: Dragon's Egg
Copyright © 2016 by Emily Martha Sorensen
Cover art by Eva Urbaníková

All rights reserved. Printed in the United States of America.

ISBN-13: 978-1536889840
ISBN-10: 1536889849

http://www.emilymarthasorensen.com

For my friend Heather,
who has been looking for years for
more clean new adult fantasy.

And for my brother Michael,
who is constantly looking
for books about dragons.

CHAPTER 1
Eggs

Rose twisted her finger through her long, piled-up hair, crumpled her hat in her hand, and stepped into the dragon wing of the Museum of Natural History, her favorite place in the whole city.

She hoped the trilobites and dragon claws would help her get up the nerve to talk to Papa. He hadn't exactly been receptive when she'd mentioned fossils before.

"Hello, Miss Palmer," Mr. Teedle greeted her. He was the curator of the dragon collection, and he knew her well. "Back again?"

"Yes." Rose hesitated. "I'm going to tell my father today."

"You don't need his permission!" Mr. Teedle said encouragingly. "It's not the nineteenth century anymore. It's 1920. Women have been paleontologists for over a hundred years!"

"I wish he understood that," Rose said, shaking her head. "I do need his permission to study geology. He pays my tuition and housing."

"I suppose he thinks you should simply get married?" Mr. Teedle asked with exasperation.

"No . . ." Rose hesitated. "It's my mother who'd like to see that. It's just that he thinks a woman's work is in the classroom."

Mr. Teedle shook his head and sighed heavily. Then he brightened. "Come see what we just brought in! It's astonishing!"

1

Rose followed him further into the room, her fears evaporating in the familiar place. A dragon's skull hung on the wall, enormous horns protruding from its head and nose. The right horn was broken, with fractures running all down it. She passed a glass case against the wall that was filled with rocks imprinted by dragon claws.

They were coming up on her favorite exhibit: two stones scorched by dragon fire, a rare treasure. There were only a few dozen around the world, and it was thought that they might represent some kind of writing system, given that the patterns seemed highly precise, yet irregular. It was hoped that these stones, or those like them, would be the key to uncovering what dragon fire had been used for, which might in turn be a clue to whether there were dragon species that had been intelligent.

It was the unanswered questions that Rose found the most fascinating. She itched to find the answers to them. She craved the thrill of discovery, and longed for the long hours of careful puzzle-solving. She envied even the assistants who did nothing but brush dirt off fossils, day after day. To be that close to newly-discovered fossils, to touch them daily, would be a dream.

And dragon fire was one of the most puzzling questions in paleontology. Nearly as puzzling as the question of whether any dragon species had been intelligent. Rose dreamed of being the one to find the answers to them.

"Here we are!" Mr. Teedle said proudly. "What do you think?"

Rose shook herself out of her reverie.

The glass case in the center of the room no longer held her favorite exhibit.

"Dragon eggs?" Rose asked, trying to hide her dismay. "What happened to the dragon fire stones?"

"On loan to The Academy of Natural Sciences," Mr. Teedle said. "These are our newest acquisition. They were uncovered in a hidden cave near the bone beds in Vernal. Aren't they something?"

Rose stared at the twelve eggs in the case. Whole dragon eggs were rare, though eggshell fragments were common.

Twelve real ones found in one place would have been quite exciting. But these were clearly *not* real dragon eggs: they were dusky orange with brown spots. Real dragon eggs would be fossilized.

"An artist's recreation. How nice," she said politely.

"They're not an artist's recreation," Mr. Teedle said excitedly. "They're not calcified at all. We're not sure what the shells are made of, as we haven't been able to shave a piece off of any of them to test. They were found by the bones of adult *Deinonychus antirrhopus* dragons, and they match the shape of fossilized eggs we have found of the species. Aren't they *something*?"

Rose's eyes widened. She stared at the eggs, riveted. "Are you quite certain they aren't fakes?"

"We haven't been able to prove that they originated in the Mesozoic Era, so no, we can't be certain. But the material they're made from doesn't seem to be one anyone is capable of fabricating."

"How do we know they're dragon eggs?" Rose blurted out. "How do we know they're not just . . . just some undiscovered reptile that lives in that part of the world?"

"Excellent question," Mr. Teedle said. "That's a hypothesis that several people have put forth. But the prevailing theory currently is that these are *Deinonychus antirrhopus* eggs, somehow preserved by a mechanism we don't understand."

"They should be decayed by now," Rose breathed. "They should be impossible."

"Well, I certainly hope they're possible, or else the museum has spent a lot of money on fakes," Mr. Teedle chuckled.

"How could the Dragon National Monument bear to part with these?" she blurted out. "Were they mad?"

"They found hundreds, all in one place," Mr. Teedle said. "The Smithsonian has bought six. The Field Museum of National History has bought eight. The Dragon National Monument has a clutch of sixty currently on display."

"Perhaps the species is still alive," Rose murmured. "Is that possible?"

"Who knows what's possible?" Mr. Teedle asked with a smile, spreading his hands. "It's an exciting time to be in paleontology."

Rose nodded emphatically.

Another patron wandered into the room from the hallway. He wore a well-worn suit with a short jacket, and carried a black fedora in his hand. His hair was oiled and slicked back, but still looked mussed, and he had no mustache, which made his face look bare. "Excuse me, is this the Hall of Ornithischian Dragons?" he asked.

"Check the signs," Mr. Teedle called back. "This is the Hall of Saurischian Dragons."

"Thank you," the man said, turning to walk out of the room.

A vision slammed into Rose's mind.

She was a tiny infant, crawling across the vast, dry landscape under a beating sun. She shivered, her whole lizardly body wriggling from head to tail. She stumbled forward, her tiny claws grasping for purchase, her tail sagging and sticky.

She wriggled around and turned back, and found herself looking back at a broken eggshell, slathered with a trail of goop after her. She smacked the dry ground with her claw and looked up, terrified.

There, high above her, were the comforting presence of her parents. She knew their minds, and their faces from what they had shown her. She opened her mouth and let out a small, shrill cry, and her mother reached out a claw and gently removed a sliver of shell that was trapping her tail.

Stumbling forward again, she at last collapsed in a heap, and her father carefully reached down to pluck her up. In the sizzling warmth of his palm, she let out a soft sigh and dozed off to sleep.

Rose gasped and returned to being human, standing in the Hall of Saurischian Dragons, right outside the case full of dragon eggs.

"Did you . . . did you . . .?" she stumbled.

"Yes," Mr. Teedle said, his eyes huge and his forehead sweaty. He ran his hand down the slick surface of his greying hair, over and over again.

Chapter 1: Eggs

"I saw it, too," the stranger said. He walked toward them and the case. "In the hot sun, slithering forward . . ."

". . . but I felt cold," Rose finished for him.

"My tail felt sagging and sticky . . ." Mr. Teedle whispered.

". . . until my mother pulled the eggshell off me," the stranger finished.

They all stared at each other.

"It wasn't *my* memory," the stranger said. "I've never hatched from an egg."

For some reason, that struck Rose as funny. She started giggling.

The stranger's eyes fell on the display right beside them. "Those eggs," he said. "Is one of those eggs alive?"

Rose fell silent. Her heart hammered. The blood rushed to her ears.

"Of course not," Mr. Teedle said. He hesitated. "At least . . . we don't *think* . . ."

They all stared at the display case. The twelve matching eggs did nothing.

CHAPTER 2
Evaluation

"One of those eggs is alive," the stranger said. "I'm sure of it."

"How can you be sure?" Rose asked skeptically.

"Those things *look* alive. The skeletons don't." The stranger waved his hand around to indicate the rest of the room. "Besides, the vision was about hatching. Where else could it have come from?"

"That's not particularly sound reasoning," Mr. Teedle said. "But it's a valid hypothesis. These are the newest addition to the room, and nothing else like that has ever happened before."

"This implies that there might be living *Deinonychus antirrhopus* in Vernal," Rose breathed. "Imagine what we could learn from a fertile egg."

"There can't be dragons still alive," the stranger objected. "People would have found evidence of it by now."

"What do you think this is?" Mr. Teedle asked.

"I think it's an egg that's survived for millions of years. Hibernating or something."

"How could an egg survive for millions of years?" Rose asked skeptically.

"How could a dragon breathe out fire without self-injury?" Mr. Teedle shrugged. "How could a dragon even produce it?

6

There are still many unanswered questions about them. Almost anything is possible."

"But this means we will be able to find out the answers," Rose breathed. "With a *live dragon* . . ."

"Hang on," the stranger objected. "If this is a live animal, it doesn't belong in a museum. It belongs in a zoo."

"I imagine there could be a collaborative project," Rose said, waving her hand carelessly. "Every scientist worth their salt will want to study it."

"Imagine what this will do for the museum," Mr. Teedle said, his eyes shining. "Imagine the prestige. Imagine the number of visitors. Imagine how many fresh expeditions this will finance."

"Imagine that this is a living creature that should have some say in where it's going to live!" the stranger shouted.

"The eggs are the property of the museum," Rose said. "I'm sure a great deal of care will be made to make proper arrangements."

"Actually, the young man has a point," Mr. Teedle said, rubbing his chin. "We don't know how intelligent *Deinonychus* dragons were, but there's a great deal of evidence that they may have been as intelligent as apes. Perhaps even as intelligent as humans."

Rose felt a thrill down her spine. There'd be an answer to that question, at long last. Someone would be able to assess the behavior of a living specimen and evaluate it. Would she have a chance of being involved in the project? Even as an observer?

"Intelligent as humans?" The stranger stared at both of them, slack-jawed. "Then this isn't an animal we're talking about at all. This is a child. A baby!"

Mr. Teedle looked troubled.

Rose wasn't sure if she should keep arguing her point, but the concern was valid, and it was worrying.

"You're right," she said. "We have to proceed on the assumption that it might be. It's silly, but harmless, to treat an animal like a person. It's potentially very harmful to treat a person like an animal."

"But it would not be very practical to proceed that way," Mr. Teedle said, rubbing his oiled hair. "The egg is, as you mentioned, the property of the museum. It might be as intelligent as humans, but it won't have the legal rights."

"If it's a person, then it needs to *get* legal rights," Rose said. "The sooner, the better."

The stranger smiled at her. "What's your name, Miss . . .?"

"Rose Palmer," Rose said. "I'm a student at Hunter College."

"Henry Wainscott. I'm a student at City College."

The men-only college with the gorgeous Gothic architecture? Rose thought. She envied him. The academic standards of his school were probably far more rigorous than her women-only college.

"Pleased to meet you, Mr. Wainscott," she said formally, holding out her hand.

He shook it.

"So we have a plan, then," Rose said briskly. "Assuming that the egg is alive, and assuming that it was the source of the vision we saw, we shall assume it is intelligent unless proven otherwise. We should probably speak with the director of the museum and see what protections can be applied right away."

She said that with a hint of hope, because she had wanted to meet the director for a long time. She knew nothing about him save what Mr. Teedle had mentioned: that he was a busy man who rarely ventured out into the museum during the hours it was open. It would be an honor to become acquainted with him.

"No, it won't do," Mr. Teedle broke in, interrupting her thoughts. "It's all very well to say that, but the egg is the property of the museum, and we paid a great deal of money to acquire it."

"You paid for *twelve* eggs, didn't you?" Henry demanded, jabbing his finger at the exhibit. "Look! You'll still have eleven!"

"And lose the most valuable artifact this museum has ever acquired? I'm sorry, but the director would not stand for that. Neither would I, I'm afraid."

"It's not an artifact, it's a baby dragon!" Henry shouted. "Stop thinking about what's good for the museum, and think about what's good for the *child!*"

8

He was saying *child* now, Rose noted. As if it were an absolute certainty.

"There's a simple way to resolve this dispute," Rose said firmly, taking a step forward as if to curtail the altercation by inserting herself between them. "We ask the egg if it is intelligent, and if there is anything it wants. Perhaps it can communicate more clearly than it has already."

"And if it doesn't?" Henry demanded.

"And if it does?" Mr. Teedle asked.

"Then we evaluate it from what it says. Perhaps the egg is intelligent. Perhaps it isn't. Perhaps the egg is content to stay in the museum, or actually wishes to be here. That's a possibility that neither of you seems to have considered."

The two men exchanged uneasy looks.

"It can't do any harm to try," Mr. Teedle said.

Henry walked over to the display case and knocked on the glass.

"Mr. Wainscott!" Mr. Teedle said sharply.

"Helloooooo," Henry said loudly, paying the curator no heed. "Hello in there! Are you the one who sent us the vision? Are you one of the dragon eggs? We want to know what you want. Can you understand me?"

A wave of memory and emotion bowled Rose over.

Why hadn't they answered before? He had given them his mother's memory of hatching. Wasn't it clear? He would give them one of his ancestors' memories. His father had given it to him.

It bubbled to the surface. It felt muted, like the original experience had been muffled by the interpretation of many minds.

She was very cramped and uncomfortable. Her legs felt powerful, but her neck was weak. Her mother and father had instructed her to strengthen her neck so that she could use the egg tooth to chip her way out, but she had been lazy.

Suddenly, there was emptiness where her father had been. She thrashed and kicked and screamed out, but only the mother's mind answered. She sunk into a deep despair. Cold filled her heart, her mind, her limbs. She fell asleep.

After a long time, a new presence in her mind dawned. It was a new father, chosen by the mother to replace the one they had lost. Uncertainty gave way to relief, and she awakened fully. She worked to strengthen her neck and burst out of the egg at last.

Rose drew a breath, but there was no time to think. Now there was a raw memory again, unfiltered from being passed through other minds.

His parents had vanished. His parents had vanished! In terror and despair, he retreated to the special sleep his parents had shown him how to do in case they vanished.

At some point, other minds came. Not his parents. He didn't want them. He refused to wake up. They went away.

There was movement. There were more minds. Sometimes many, mostly two minds at once. Every so often, he woke up. But he never liked them, so he always went back to sleep.

There were no minds at all for a very long time. The emptiness was so complete, consciousness faded entirely. All sense of time was lost.

His mother's mind was there.

He jerked awake, disoriented, but it wasn't her mind. It was good, though. Similar. Where was his father's mind? He couldn't hatch without them both. He wouldn't! Maybe he would go back to sleep.

There it was! His father's mind! He exulted, waiting for the minds to greet him, but they didn't. The father's mind was going away. No!

Didn't they know he was here? He'd give them the memory of his mother's hatching so they would understand.

They didn't answer. They didn't answer. They didn't answer. Why didn't they answer?

They had to stay. They had to raise him. Didn't they know the rules?

The memory ended, and Rose drew in a breath, gasping. Her heart was filled with terror, and her arms were shaking.

CHAPTER 3
Experience

Henry stood there, frozen, shell-shocked.

"I have to go," he blurted out. He started to back out of the room.

"Wait," Mr. Teedle said. "Why —?"

"I have to go, too." Rose scrambled away from the case, terror lancing through her mind like jagged rips of lightning. "I'll be back — be back — thanks, Mr. Teedle."

She turned and fled after Henry, racing down the stairs from the fourth floor. She nearly bumped into another patron ascending in her haste.

"Wait!" Mr. Teedle shouted after her. "What did you see?"

Rose leapt down the last few stairs and raced for the exit. In blind terror, she ducked under the arm of someone opening the door to the museum and raced down the street. Tears stung at her eyes. So desperate — terrified — so lonely —

Central Park was across the street. Rose slowed while cars drove past, her heart hammering. Those weren't her memories. Those weren't her feelings. Those weren't her loneliness, her desperation.

But it was her terror.

Her arms were shaking, she realized numbly. She must look dreadful right now. What must people be thinking?

11

Maybe she should have stopped to tell Mr. Teedle what the dragon had said. Maybe she should have explained.

But she couldn't face going back. Not in the face of such desperate need. She waited for a gap in traffic, and then crossed the street into Central Park, her mind numb as she took in the late summer's afternoon.

Two women passed her pushing prams. They chattered to each another as a small child trailed after one of them. It was impossible to tell what gender the small child was, as the child was wearing a sailor suit with an overlong blouse, and she couldn't tell if there were shorts or skirt underneath. Most likely a boy, as the sailor suit was pink. But you never knew.

A woman sat on the grass nearby, watching two small boys wrestle with a huge dog. A third boy ran over, waving a shredded scrap of cloth, and the dog lunged for it, snapping excitedly. The boys screamed with laughter.

Rose glanced out over the Lake, where a couple drifted by on a boat. The woman wore a ruffled blue dress and held a flower-shaped paper parasol over her head, the black feather at the top of her hat tickling it. The man was wearing a green belted suit and a hat with a ribbon around it. At first Rose thought they were alone, and then she noticed the man was clutching a small baby in the crook of his arm.

There are so many parents around, Rose thought, swallowing. She'd never noticed it before, but children were everywhere. She walked slowly down the path, feeling a breeze whip the skirt around her ankles. *All out here with their children.*

Would a dragon child even be allowed in Central Park? No one knew when they first started to breathe fire. Perhaps a dragon child would be dangerous.

No, no, no. She couldn't even fathom having a human child yet. She wanted to study dragons, not raise one.

She started to pass by a man sitting under a tree, twisting his hat in his hands, and did a double-take as she recognized his clothing.

12

"Mr. Wainscott," she said. "What are you doing here?"

He looked up. "Miss Palmer," he said. His voice was strained. "Did you get the same message I did?"

"He wants . . ." Rose's voice faltered. She swallowed, gathered her skirt, and sat down in the shade beside him. "He wants me to be his parent."

She couldn't bring herself to say the word *mother.* Somehow, that seemed much more personal. More alien. More not-what-she'd-intended-for-her-life-path-at-all. Sure, there were some women who had children at eighteen, but she had never wanted to be one of them. She wasn't ready for that kind of commitment. How could the dragon ask such a thing?

"He wants me to be his father," Henry said.

"I can't do it," Rose blurted out. "It's an outrageous demand."

"Children aren't known for being undemanding," Henry said. "Just ask my brother. He has six-year-old twins."

"I can't do it," Rose said. "I won't do it!"

Henry was silent as he picked at the grass.

"At least we know for sure that he's intelligent," he said. "He thinks we're the equivalent of his parents."

"We don't know for sure that's what it means," Rose said, but her heart wasn't in it.

It might not be objectively sound, but the dragon had felt intelligent. Frighteningly intelligent. She didn't know of any human baby who could think so clearly. Though perhaps that was simply because she had never had the opportunity to compare: human babies lacked the ability to communicate telepathically.

"I had a professor last semester who brought up the question," Henry said. "He said they couldn't have been because there was no evidence of any written language."

"That was Edward Cope's argument," Rose snorted. "As if there haven't been human societies with no written languages! I much prefer Mary Anning's hypothesis. She said that dragons might have used scorched stones as a method of recording information, since the structure of their throats and jaws suggests that they had multiple glands for controlling the temperature of their fire and the chemicals that produced it. In the same way that some animals used scent to communicate, dragons may have been so sensitive to temperature differentials that they could use them as a form of language —"

She stopped, seeing Henry watch her with a smile on his face.

"What?" she asked.

"You're very smart, aren't you?" he asked.

"I'm very interested in the subject," Rose said, a little embarrassed.

Henry grinned. "I guess we know the answer to whether they had a written language now, too."

"We do?" Rose asked quizzically.

"Sure. This means that dragons didn't need a written language to record information permanently. They just passed down memories directly."

"No, no, no." Rose waved her hand. "That would be no more than a sophisticated oral tradition, which means it would still be colored by interpretation every generation. That doesn't mean there was no written language. We'll have to see if the dragon has any memories from ancestors that would be relevant to other questions about dragon society, or whether all that was communicated to him were memories of hatching. It would be amazing to interview him —"

"Miss Palmer," Henry interrupted. "You're very smart, but you're being very dense."

"What?" Rose faltered.

Henry sighed heavily. "This is a baby, remember? His primary concerns will be food, drink, and loving parents. He's not going to be receptive to being interviewed, especially by someone who apparently plans to reject his request."

Oh. Rose swallowed. She'd almost forgotten that, in the heat of her excitement.

"What should I do, then?" she asked in a small voice. "I don't — I don't want to be a parent right now. You can't ask that of me. That's too much to ask."

14

"I'm not asking it," Henry said. "He did."

"I still can't do it," Rose said. "I just — I just can't."

"Don't justify yourself to me," Henry said. "He's the one you owe an answer to."

Rose wrapped her arms around her knees. A breeze picked up and tried to snatch her hat off, but she grabbed it in time. She began to twist it around in her hands, as Henry had been doing earlier.

"If this had only happened a few years later," she said, "I might have been in a better position to say yes."

"Children aren't known for their spectacular timing, either," Henry said dryly. "Ask my sister-in-law how many times she got woken up at three am to change horrendous diapers of two screaming babies."

"Are you going to accept?" Rose asked, looking up at him.

Henry pondered for a moment. He ran his fingers through the grass. "Yes," he said at last. "I think I am."

"How?" Rose asked in amazement. "How can you be prepared to do that?"

"I like children," Henry said. "I've always wanted to have them. This isn't quite the way I had anticipated it happening, and it's not ideal, but . . . he chose me. He rejected hundreds of dragon parents, but he chose me. That's quite appealing."

Rose squeezed her hat tightly. Her thumbnails dug into the brim. To her that didn't seem appealing at all. It seemed terrifying. What would it be like to fail, under all that pressure? What would it cost to succeed?

CHAPTER 4
Essence

"The dragon must be waiting for an answer," Henry said, standing up. "He's likely frantic by now. I would be, if I were in his position. I'd better go."

Rose watched him walk off, his stride sure and purposeful, and it seemed incomprehensible to her. How could he be so sure of his choice after barely half an hour? Was he the sort who made decisions quickly?

She wasn't. She didn't enjoy adapting to new situations. And this one was too overwhelming for words.

You owe the dragon an answer, Rose told herself, trying to breathe slowly and think rationally. *Think about it. What are you going to say?*

Rose picked at the brim of her hat while she thought.

There were all kinds of good reasons why she couldn't do what he was asking. If she listed them one by one, maybe he would understand.

First: she was too young to be a mother. Not in an absolute sense, certainly, because there were many married women with small children her age. But she didn't feel mature enough or wise enough now. Maybe she never would. Parenthood had always been an abstract, something to consider in the future, not a priority to anticipate this year.

Second: she had her future to consider. It would be hard enough to be taken seriously right now, given her gender. If she had a child in tow, it would make her even less attractive a prospect for hiring.

A small voice in her head said, *Although maybe you could use him as a way to get hired, given his species . . .*

No. Rose shook her head. She couldn't think in those terms. She hated it when people saw her as a woman first, and a scientist second. To accept him because of his species would be atrocious hypocrisy, not to mention an atrocious reason to become a parent.

Third, then: she was too biased. It would be hard for her to resist the fascination of his species to see the person within. She'd have to work hard at it. It would be better for him to have somebody who wasn't interested in dragons.

Fourth: she had no experience with babies. None of her acquaintances or friends had children, and her cousins were all younger than her. She had two younger sisters, but they were both close enough to her in age that she could barely remember what they had been like as small children.

Fifth: she had no *interest* in babies.

That might be a logical fallacy, her rational mind prodded. *Didn't you just declare it would be better for him to have somebody who wasn't interested in dragons? By the same logic, someone who had no interest in babies would be better suited to raise them.*

Rose waved the thought off irritably. That was different. The dragon would have people treating him as nothing but a member of his species for his entire life. He needed somebody who would scarcely notice it.

Sixth. Sixth . . .

There had to be a sixth reason. There had to be a whole host of them.

Ah, yes. Sixth: he had to see that it would be far better to have parents who were married to each other than two strangers who had never met in their lives.

If she didn't accept, Henry and the dragon could pick out some other woman at their own pace. Any woman would do. Any woman would be better at it than her.

Seventh, Rose thought firmly, *there are five million people in this city. It doesn't have to be me. No matter how much like your birth mother I seem to you.*

Although that raised a question.

Why *did* she remind him of his birth mother?

Eighth, Rose thought hesitantly . . .

It was no good. Now that she was wondering, she couldn't concentrate on anything else. A familiar feeling of insatiable curiosity crawled up her spine and settled fixedly in her mind.

She had to know the answer to that. She had to.

Surely there couldn't have been that much in common between them. There were so many objections, so many reasons she didn't want a child right now. Not to mention that his mother had lived millions of years ago, in another civilization. The dragon had been sure his mother loved him, and Rose didn't know how to love a child.

Restlessly, Rose stood up. The only person who could answer that question was the dragon. She marched down the path back towards the museum, determined to find out. She entered the museum and walked up the stairs.

When she reached the top of the stairs, she walked around the bend to the Hall of Saurischian Dragons, where she spied Henry standing by the display case, speaking in soothing tones, while Mr. Teedle hovered nervously behind him.

"Miss Palmer!" Mr. Teedle said with some relief, running over to her. He ran his hand through his hair and wiped his sweaty brow. "Mr. Wainscott refuses to explain to me what's going on, and the dragon has been throwing a fit. I think I have a decent idea what a *Deinonychus antirrhopus* dragon roar must have sounded like, because the egg has been projecting memories of it across the room since you left. I had to clear the hall because the patrons were complaining! He only stopped when Mr. Wainscott came back! What happened?"

Chapter 4: Essence

"I'll explain to you later," Rose said. "I need to go talk to the dragon egg n—"

"William, don't lick the wall, that's disgusting!" a chubby woman shouted from the hallway to three children who were wandering around her. "George, stop making that noise. Leslie —"

"Excuse me! I'm sorry!" Mr. Teedle said, hurrying over. "I'm sorry, ma'am, but this room is closed. Would you please make your way over to the Hall of Ornithischian Dragons instead?"

"What? But we were just there," the woman protested. "George wants to see the *Tyrannosaurus rex*."

"I want to be one when I grow up," a fat-cheeked boy informed him, flapping his arms. "I want to fly like they did."

"*Tyrannosaurus* dragons didn't fly; the wings were vestigial," Mr. Teedle said. "If you'd like to see a flying dragon, we have a lovely *Stegosaurus stenops* on display in the Hall of Ornithischian Dragons —"

"I wanna see the T-rex! I wanna see the T-rex!" the boy shouted, hopping up and down in rage.

"We came all the way here because he had to see his favorite dragon," the boy's mother said huffily. "There's no sign saying this hall is closed. Why can't we just —"

While the two were arguing, Rose slipped away to the display case with the *Deinonychus antirrhopus* eggs. Henry was still talking to them in quiet tones.

"No, I can't speak for her," he was saying. "Yes, it would be nice to all be a family together. No, you'll have to ask her that question, not me."

"I'm here now," Rose said.

A feeling of joy burst up from the display case. The dragon sent her a flash of bubbly, happy memory of Henry's mind returning, and then a similar memory of his father returning from hunting — had that been a *Tenontosaurus?*

Rose shook her head. No. The dragon's memories of his father, or the tantalizing glimpse of a *Tenontosaurus tilletti* from the shard of his father's memory that had been included, were not important right now.

"You told us I reminded you of your mother," Rose said. "Why?"

A feeling of confusion bubbled up from the display case.

Rose tucked a strand of hair behind her ear, and tried a different approach. "Can you show me what your mother was like?"

A mix of eagerness and sadness, and then —

She was picking up several rock specimens carefully in her claws and sorting them according to classification. Some of them would be suitable for public display in the vast rock collection cave later.

And then —

She was irritated that a feathered pest had interrupted her work. She wasn't hungry, so she swiped it away with her tail. Her father, who had flown by despite all her wishes, informed her that she should have kept the thing for later. She wished he'd mind his own business and leave her alone.

And then —

The seasons had changed. She hated change. It always made her grumpy. She flicked the egg with her tail to get him to stop asking the same question for the billionth time, and wondered if the child had gotten the same maddeningly inquisitive nature that had made her parents so incessantly weary with her.

Her husband rolled the egg over with his claw and sleepily explained the answer to the question for the billionth time.

And then —

The egg was crying silently, forcefully. It was the first time his father had left to hunt since the child had gotten old enough to wake up. He had been a surprise, this baby, much earlier than she had wanted, but she'd get used to him. Perhaps she shouldn't let him know she thought him a pest sometimes. Quiet, quiet now, little one . . .

The flashes of memory ended.

Rose burst out into hysterical giggles. The dragon child was right: the two of them had been extremely alike.

CHAPTER 5
Element

So . . . . did he answer your question?" Henry asked. His hands twisted a little, like he was nervous. Perhaps he was.

"He did," Rose giggled. Why couldn't she stop laughing? "Perhaps you ought to ask why you remind him of his father."

Henry shook his head. "No, thanks. I'd rather not live in the shadow of somebody I can never replace."

For some reason, that struck Rose as hilarious, and she let out a long spurt of laughter.

"What's so funny?" Henry asked. "What did he show you?"

"Oh, he just — it's just — I — I don't know!" Rose started to cry. It came out in choking sobs.

Henry stared at her in real alarm now. "Miss Palmer!"

"It's no problem! I'm fine! I just — I — I — I —" Rose burst into sobs again.

Henry drew back in horror.

You're hysterical, the part of Rose's mind that was still rational informed her. *Calm down. Stop being so emotional. Think rationally.*

Rose drew in a deep breath and managed to clamp down on her feelings. Her arms shook, but when she spoke, her voice sounded passably steady.

21

"His mother and I were very alike," she said. "Including having the same doubts and worries. She was out of her element, too. But she loved him."

Hysteria threatened to bubble up again, so she clamped down on her feelings tightly.

Rational, she told herself sternly. *What would be the rational thing to do?*

Most of her objections had been effectively rebutted. All the ones that were left seemed selfish and whiny.

Logically, if his mother had loved him . . . then she could, too.

"All right," Rose said, her voice cracking a little. "All right. I'll do it. You win, demanding brat."

Henry stared at her in astonishment. "First you outright plan on rejecting him . . . and then *that's* how you accept?"

"It's good enough for him," Rose said. The faintest hint of terror leaked through her mental shield, so she clamped down on it hard, clenching her fists as she did so. "His original mother would have said the same thing."

"Your hands are shaking," Henry said. "Are you sure you're all right?"

I never said I was, Rose thought. She breathed in deeply, and then breathed out again. The shaking in her hands quelled.

"I'll need time to get used to it," she said. "I will be."

The dragon's mind bounced with excitement. He was going to hatch and be with his new mother and father, who were just like his old ones. They would teach him how to run and fly and play, and they would all soar off together —

"Hold on," Rose said. "We're human. We can't fly. You're going to need to understand that."

— and it would be so much fun! Hatching was a while away, but he would grow nice and strong so that he could burst out and they'd all breathe fire together —

"We're human," Henry said. "We don't breathe fire."

— and his father would teach him how to hunt those tasty meat creatures he brought home, crunch crunch —

Chapter 5: Element

"I don't think he understands," Henry said with exasperation.

"How can he?" Rose said. "He's never seen a human before. He's never seen *anything* before, except through another dragon's memories."

— and he could hardly wait to stretch out his tail, and they would teach him to swipe things with it!

"He's in for a world of disappointment, isn't he?" Henry sighed.

"Maybe not," Rose said. She felt a tentative brush of anticipation. "For a curious child, a world unlike anything in his ancestors' memories might be wonderful and fascinating."

Crunch crunch! The dragon sent them memories of the noise his father made while eating. Crunch crunch!

Henry shuddered.

"You realize he's a carnivorous dragon," Rose said with amusement. "We're going to be hearing a lot of that. For that matter, we're going to need to figure out what he can eat."

Henry rubbed the side of his face. "That's going to be really expensive, isn't it?"

Rose felt a little perverse satisfaction that he hadn't thought everything through before he'd agreed. "Unless he can eat primarily rats and pigeons."

Crunch crunch!

"Stop that!" Henry shouted. "That's enough of that noise, thank you!"

His new father didn't like the noise. That was strange, because his old father had made that noise. He'd share a new noise his old father had made.

"What is that sound?!" Henry yelped, putting his hands over his ears, as if that would help. "It sounds like nails on a chalkboard!"

Rose barely kept her face straight. She was glad she wasn't the only one who was out of their element. "I think it's his father sharpening his claws on a rock."

Henry squished his fingers against the glass of the display case. "That is NOT AN IMPROVEMENT," he said. "NO MORE NOISES."

"Excuse me," a very cold voice said from behind them. "Please don't touch the glass."

Rose spun around to see Mr. Teedle standing by a man she didn't know who emanated an air of condescending authority. His suit was very well-tailored, and he held an elegant, matching derby hat in one hand, and an ornamental cane in the other.

"Oh," Henry said, taking his hand away from the glass and turning around. "I'm sorry, sir. I'm afraid we haven't had the pleasure of being introduced?"

"My name is Director Campbell," the man said coldly. "I am in charge of this museum. Teedle wanted to acquaint me with the dragon eggs. He claims that one of them is alive. What is this tomfoolery?"

"It's not tomfoolery," Henry said hastily. "He *is* alive. We were just talking with him when you came in."

"Talking with a dragon egg," the director said in a flat voice. "How charming. And I suppose next, you will have a conversation with the *Tyrannosaurus* skeleton?"

"That wouldn't do much good, seeing as a skeleton's not alive," Henry said with evident annoyance.

"Neither are fossilized eggs," the director said in a clipped voice. He paused, flicking his gaze over to the display case. "Forgive me. Un-fossilized eggs, but ones that are still at least one hundred million years old."

"Director." Mr. Teedle cleared his throat. "One of those eggs does seem to be alive. I have experienced it. That's why I brought you here. It seems to have some kind of telepathy. It showed visions of its ancestors' memories to us, and then it made a mental version of a roaring noise. All of the patrons in this hall heard it, which is why I had to clear it out. I'm sure the egg can share some memories with you, too, director. They're quite fascinating."

Rose recognized a cue.

"Dragon?" she asked, turning around. "Would you please share a memory with everyone in this room?"

Chapter 5: Element

He was sullen. His new father didn't like his noises. He was going to take a nap.

"No, don't *sleep!*" Henry cried.

Nothing.

Rose swallowed. She had always wanted to meet the director of the museum. Looking like a fool was not the way she'd hoped to do it.

CHAPTER 6
Entrance

Wat kind of joke are you trying to pull?" the director demanded. "Teedle, if this is something you are in on, I'm not amused."

You don't look like you have much of a sense of humor about anything, Rose thought. But she said nothing. She couldn't blame the man for being offended. The story sounded crazy, and it was unreasonable to expect him to believe such an outlandish claim without evidence.

"I'm sorry to have wasted your time," she said, bowing her head. "The dragon will, perhaps, offer communication to you another time. My apologies for this inconvenience."

"Actually, we need to talk to you about something," Henry said.

Rose's head shot up. *What are you doing?*

"What would that be?" the director asked frostily.

"The egg," Henry said. "It can't stay here. This isn't an appropriate environment for a living being."

Rose stared at him in horror. *Are you out of your wits?*

The director stared at him with absolute incredulity. "And I suppose you'd like to take it off our hands and move it to a more appropriate location?"

"Exactly," Henry said, looking pleased. "Miss Palmer and I will take care of it jointly."

"I suppose that's you," the director said sharply, looking at Rose. "What do you have to say?"

Rose was silent, gripping her hands into fists.

"Sir," she said at last, keeping her voice level, "we believe this dragon has petitioned us to be his caretakers. We humbly ask for your permission to be present at all important events relating to his care and hatching."

She purposefully did not use the word *parents*, though the dragon's meaning had been clear. That word would only cause the man to think she was a sentimental female who thought of nothing but marrying and babies.

The director gave her a narrow-eyed, measured look.

"If the dragon does not hatch, of course, I ask for no more than what any patron of the museum would: to visit the egg regularly, not to touch it or to interfere with the exhibits in any way. When the dragon does hatch, I ask to be present, to be a part of the studying, and in anything further, for the dragon's preferences to be weighed."

The director's eyebrows softened. He looked suspicious, but not nearly as angry as before.

"To suggest that a creature could hatch after millions of years is ludicrous," he said. "There's simply no good reason it could happen."

"Yes," Rose agreed. "But if it should, imagine what can be learned about the species."

The director looked thoughtful.

Rose's heart pounded.

"Your point is well-made," he said. "Very well. I see no reason why you cannot visit regularly, just so long as you pay the entry fee and don't disrupt the other patrons' visits. And if the creature does hatch, not that I believe such a thing will happen, I will consider your request to be present at the event."

Rose fought to keep the joy from showing up on her face. *I did it!* she exulted. *We'll have all the access we need!*

"That's not enough, sir," Henry said bluntly.

Rose stared at him in horror. *What are you doing?*

"That dragon — velociraptor or whatever it is — is far more than just a species. This is an individual, with very definite wants and needs."

"*Deinonychus antirrhopus*," Rose murmured, humiliated. "*Velociraptor mongoliensis* were tiny."

"Whatever," Henry said, waving his hand, as if that had no bearing. "The dragon's telepathic, and plainly intelligent. Leaving him in the museum, away from his parents and surrounded by nothing but corpses, would be cruelty."

"Well, unluckily for it, all other *Deinonychus antirrhopus* dragons are dead," the director said sharply.

"Yes, but *we* are his new parents," Henry said sharply. "That's my son in that display case, and I demand to take him home with me."

The director stood very stiffly and said nothing.

"Mr. Wainscott!" Rose hissed. "May I please talk to you?"

Henry ignored her. And, incredibly, he actually managed to make things worse.

"I don't know which one is our egg," he said, "so we should probably pick them all up, shake them around, see if that wakes him up —"

"Disregard all that!" Rose said, breaking in desperately. "We've no intention of disturbing any of your very valuable and well-cared-for exhibits. Mr. Wainscott, we should go."

"I'm not going anywhere until I have my son," Henry said stubbornly. "How do you think he's going to feel when he wakes up and he finds we're not here? Not to mention that the museum will be closed tomorrow. We can't leave him alone for a day and a half. That's unpardonable!"

"You know what is unpardonable?" the director said with cool composure. "This blatant effrontery and abominable rudeness."

"Let's go," Rose said, pulling on Henry's sleeve.

He shook her off angrily. "You think that was rude?" he demanded. "I can be rude. Let me tell you what I think of someone who thinks it's all right to keep a child from his parents."

Then he began to let loose a string of insults that would have made a sailor blush. In desperation, Rose slapped her hand over his mouth.

The director looked at Mr. Teedle in amazement. "Is he out of his senses?"

"Apparently so," Mr. Teedle said, looking weary. "Mr. Wainscott, there is no way you are taking any exhibit out of this museum, living or not. I will make sure to explain to the dragon egg the situation before we close for the day."

"I'll tell him myself," Henry said, ripping Rose's hand off his mouth, "because if he's not leaving, neither am I."

"Oh, aren't you?" the director asked.

The doors slammed shut behind them with a whoosh of finality. Inside, a burly security guard eyed them through the glass, his arms folded menacingly.

"You got me kicked out, too!" Rose snarled. "Why did you do that? *Why?* Do you have any idea how stupid you were? Learn to compromise!"

"But I was right!" Henry protested.

Rose shoved her hat on her head and glared at him. *How could any woman with a personality like mine have married an idiot like this?*

"Don't worry," Henry said, eyeing the grandeur of the pillars on either side of them. "There must be a way to get back into the building. Maybe I could break one of those windows, or . . ."

"Mr. Wainscott," Rose said with extreme exasperation, "I believe you have caused enough disasters for today. Please try not to get yourself arrested by destroying or intruding on private property. Rest assured that if you intend to try, I would be the first to report you to the authorities."

"It wouldn't work, anyway," Henry murmured, putting his hat back on. "I'm sure they have security guards at night."

"If that's your primary concern, I remain apprehensive," Rose said icily. "Mr. Wainscott, negotiations would have been possible in a few days, after it had become evident the child was alive and requesting our presence. Now, you have poisoned the director's goodwill. I am not pleased."

Henry's shoulders drooped.

Without a word, Rose turned on her heel and walked away.

CHAPTER 7
Excuse

It wasn't just that he had gotten her thrown out of the museum, Rose reflected as she walked down the street, swinging her arms fiercely as her heels clicked against the sidewalk. If she were truly honest with herself, she would admit that she was glad for the excuse to leave the dragon there for as long as possible.

Normally a person has time to acquaint themselves with the idea that they are going to raise a child, Rose thought. *Surely it is not unreasonable for me to be glad it wasn't reasonable to bring him home today.*

Not to mention the exhausting question of whether she or Henry would have been the one to bring the egg home. That was a question she would rather leave for another day, too. She had roommates, and she didn't know how she would explain the situation to them when she didn't even know how to sort through it herself.

Rose turned a corner out of habit, and then realized she should have turned the other direction, towards her family's house instead of her apartment. She turned around and nearly bumped into Henry.

"Mr. Wainscott!" she cried, startled. "Were you following me?"

"No! Well, yes. I figured I should apologize to you. And maybe we should talk about what we're going to do."

"Very well," Rose said, folding her arms. "Apologize."

"You're not going to make this easy on me, are you?"

Rose stared at him frostily.

Henry sighed. "All right. I'm sorry. I might have gotten overexcited. I told you I love children, right?"

"I believe you mentioned it."

"I *hate* it when children cry. He was in a panicked frenzy by the time I got back. The thought of leaving him alone for a day and a half, without being able to comfort him . . ."

"He's currently in an egg," Rose said flatly. "There will be plenty of time to coddle him and allow him to be clingy. Have a little patience."

"I'm trying to apologize!" Henry cried.

"Then apologize, don't make excuses."

"I'm sorry," Henry said huffily. "I'm sorry that we got kicked out of the museum. I'm sorry the director got mad. Happy?"

"You've just said you're sorry about the consequences of your actions. You've said nothing about your actions. That still doesn't constitute an apology."

Henry glowered at her.

Rose walked around him and continued towards her family's house.

"All right, I'm sorry!" Henry said, running after her. "I'm sorry I got hotheaded and didn't leave well enough alone!"

"Thank you," Rose said, stopping to glance back at him. "That's an apology." She resumed walking.

Henry trotted after her. "So . . . why are you still walking away?"

"I'm not walking away," Rose said. "I'm late. If you want to talk, we'll have to talk on the way."

"Late to what?" Henry asked.

"Dinner with my family. My mother insists on it every week."

"Oh." Henry walked on silently for awhile. "Should I meet your family?" he asked hesitantly. "Given the circumstances . . ."

"I suppose you could," Rose said, increasing the pace.

It occurred to her that the later she was, the fouler a mood her father would be in. She still had to talk to him about changing her classes next semester. "Don't mention the egg."

"Why not mention the egg?" Henry asked, hurrying to keep up with her.

"Because the story would sound mad, and it would only complicate the conversation we need to have tonight. It would be best if my father isn't in a bad mood. He'd be apt to refuse."

"Oh, right," Henry said. "Of course."

It wasn't long before they reached her family's house. Rose rang the doorbell, hoping her father was in a patient mood.

Her mother opened the door. She wore an old-fashioned shawl bedecked with flowers, and a lovely blue dinner gown that looked like it had seen better days. Rose's mother's taste in clothing was quite nice, but the budget her parsimonious husband gave her was quite slim. She spent most of her effort in making sure her three daughters were properly dressed, in the hopes that they would all land suitable husbands quickly.

"Rose!" her mother cried, throwing out her arms and embracing her. "We wondered where you were. Your papa's quite annoyed that you're late."

"I'm sorry," Rose said. "I was . . . delayed."

"Hello," Henry said from behind her, reaching out his hand. "Would you be Rose's mother? My name is Henry Wainscott. I'm Rose's fiancé."

What? Rose spun around and gaped at him. *What in the world is he saying?!*

"Oh," Rose's mother gasped. "I — I never even heard that Rose had a beau — George! George, you'll never believe who Rose brought with her! You'll never believe what they said!"

She ran into the house, leaving the door wide open.

"Why would you say that?!" Rose hissed incredulously. "We're not engaged!"

"I thought we were!" Henry whispered. "We agreed to be parents to the same child, and you said you wanted to talk to your father —"

"About my *tuition!*"

"Well, you might have *said* that!"

"What's this?" Rose's father asked, stomping to the doorway. "My daughter brought a fiancé to see me?"

"Henry Wainscott, sir," Henry said, holding out his hand awkwardly. "Uh . . . I may have been a bit premature . . ."

"You certainly were," Rose's father growled. "You haven't asked my permission yet. Don't just stand there, come in!"

Henry shot Rose a panicked look.

"You heard the man," she said tightly.

Henry removed his hat and ran his hand over his oiled hair nervously. He stepped into the parlor, twisting the hat around in his hands.

"You're engaged?!" Rose's sisters gasped, barreling down the stairs. One of them wore fluffy yellow and the other wore fluffy blue. They were only nine months apart in age, and nearly interchangeable.

"Hello, Sara. Hello, Louise," Rose said flatly.

Louise, the one in the blue dress, squealed and held her hands to her chest. "How did you meet? Was it love at first sight?"

Sara pretended to swoon, and Louise caught her.

"We met at the Museum of Natural History," Rose said.

"That place?" Rose's father asked sharply. "Were you wasting your allowance on those blasted bones again?"

Rose set her jaw. This was not a good beginning.

"I know, I know!" Sara cried. "One of them fell on a dragon skull, and it was love at first *bite!*" She made a chomping sound.

Louise giggled.

"I'm so glad that Rose has a beau!" their mother trilled, coming out of the kitchen with a platter of ham and onions that were all rather scorched at the edges. "Here I thought we'd never see her be interested in anything but those dusty books!"

"She's a terrible cook, by the way," Sara informed Henry. "She forgets there's something on the stove and burns it."

"I haven't done that in months," Rose objected. She didn't mention her roommates had nearly banned her from the kitchen.

34

Chapter 7: Excuse

"Hush!" Rose's mother said, shooing the girls away with a slightly panicked look. "Don't scare him away! Shoo! Shoo!"

Henry was chuckling in amusement when Rose's father loomed up behind him.

"So?" the man thundered. He snatched Henry's hat and tossed it at the hat rack. It snagged the hook and spun around slightly, then stayed put. "Why don't you tell me the reasons you think you should marry my daughter?"

Henry swallowed visibly.

CHAPTER 8
Engaged

Don't mention the dragon egg, Rose thought. *Do not mention the dragon egg. Just find a graceful way to get out of it, and then leave.*

"To tell you the truth, sir," Henry said, his fingers twisting nervously, "there's no good reason why I should marry your daughter. We've only known each other for a short time. I've liked her since we first met . . ."

Sara and Louise giggled.

"Shhhh!" Rose's mother hissed, waving them down and watching Henry avidly.

". . . but really," Henry faltered, "I couldn't blame you if you wanted to refuse me. I'll go now."

He tried to get to the hat rack, but Rose's father blocked his escape.

"Hang on now," the man said. "It would do Rose some good to be married. Teach her to be more realistic about things."

Rose's jaw clenched.

"Tell me about yourself, boy," Rose's father said. "What do you do?"

"Uh . . . I'm a sophomore at City College. I study biology."

"That's a good field to be in," Rose's father said. "Good way to earn a living."

36

Chapter 8: Engaged

Excuse me? Rose thought indignantly. *You wouldn't let me take the biology class I wanted to this semester!*

Henry murmured something noncommittal.

"You should go into medicine," Rose's father said firmly. "There's always work for doctors."

"My father says the same thing," Henry said wearily.

"Smart man," Rose's father approved.

"Yes, I think the two of you would get along," Henry sighed.

"To the table, to the table!" Rose's mother said, gesturing. "We're already late with starting! Who wants to say grace?"

"I will!" Louise volunteered. And then she said something so short and covered in giggles that nobody could understand a word of it.

". . . Right," Rose's father said, after a pause. He cleared his throat and reached for the butter knife and a roll. "So, how do you plan to support my daughter?"

"I . . . have no plans, sir. I know that must be a problem. We must have been too hasty. How about you forget what I said before, and I can come back later . . ." He got up from his chair.

Rose's father grabbed his arm and shoved him back down. "How are you paying for your rent now?" he demanded. "Do you live with your parents?"

"N-no, I have a stipend from my grandfather," Henry stammered. "It covers my tuition and living expenses until I graduate."

"Ah." Rose's father sat back in satisfaction. "So you *do* have some means. Good. I assume that getting married wouldn't cause a problem there?"

Henry shook his head. "My older brother got married during his senior year, and it wasn't a problem. But, uh, sir —"

Rose's father plowed right on. "Now, tell me about your classes. I assume you're getting good grades?"

"I was at the top of all my classes this semester," Rose said sourly. "Thank you for asking, Papa."

"Oh, look at how fun this is!" Rose's mother put in bubbily. "It's so nice to have another man around! George loves a solid intellectual discussion, and he never gets them around here!"

Rose's fists tightened on her lap.

"Rose strikes me as quite intellectual," Henry said.

"That's why she's going into teaching," Rose's father said, wiping his knife clean of butter and taking a large bite out of his roll. "Or was. Won't be necessary now that she's getting married, eh?"

Rose's fists were clenched so tightly, her arms started shaking. If this meant her father tried to pull her out of college altogether, she would never forgive Henry.

"Oh, no," Henry said, some sharpness in his voice. "I'm sure she'll want to keep studying. In fact, I'd say it's a *necessity*. I certainly wouldn't want to marry a woman who gave up on her schooling."

Rose's father looked rather taken aback.

"When are you going to get married?" Rose's mother asked excitedly. "Have you chosen a date?"

"I'll have to discuss that with Rose," Henry said vaguely. He flicked a glance over at her.

Rose kept her face still, betraying no emotion.

"We should try for late spring," Rose's mother said, her eyes bright. "You know what they say about June brides."

"That's up to Rose," Henry said.

Rose fixed her gaze on the hideous cubist painting her father had bought last year. It was hanging on the wall where her mother's oil pastel picture of squirrels used to sit. Her mother's choice had been a trivial thing, amateur work, but Rose had loved it. The two squirrels fighting over one acorn while several more hung on a branch above them had reminded her of her sisters.

Then Rose's father had come home with a painting he had bought at a gallery, one with jagged edges, garish colors, and a hefty price tag. Now she was forced to stare at it every time she ate dinner with her family.

"Excuse me," Henry said, pushing back his chair. "Would you mind if I excuse myself for a minute? I'd like some air."

"You want to smoke?" Rose's father asked. "I have cigars."

Chapter 8: Engaged

"No, thank you," Henry said. "There's something I'd like to speak with Rose about. Rose? Would you mind coming with me?"

Rose pushed her chair back and got up, her face still and her voice silent. She followed Henry to the front door, which he opened. They went outside and stood on the front step, and he shut the door.

"I'm sorry," he said. "I really thought you were thinking the same thing. This is a sincere apology."

There was a rustle and thump on the other side of the door.

"Speak quietly," Rose said. "My sisters are listening in."

Henry eyed the door. "People do that?"

"*Constantly.*"

Henry rubbed his forehead, then his bare upper lip. He looked uncertain of what to say.

Rose stood there for a moment in silence, looking at him. He wasn't wrong that getting married was the logical thing to do. She simply hadn't thought about it. The thought of marrying a stranger was not terribly appealing, but the thought of splitting a child between two households wasn't appealing, either.

Then again, the thought of marrying purely for logic was . . . fairly depressing. Besides, she'd already chosen to make one lifelong commitment today. Two was far too many. The man also had several annoying qualities. She wasn't sure she wanted him in her life permanently.

Not that it would be easy to avoid that in any case, since they'd both agreed to raise the dragon.

So the real question is, Rose thought, *do I think someone better will come along that I'd regret not being able to marry?*

Rose surveyed him silently. He wasn't unattractive. He seemed like a decent man, and one who respected her. There were things about him that were maddening, but that would probably be true about anyone. Unless some terrible secret came to light, he was as good a prospect as any.

"I'll consider it," she said.

"Consider what?" Henry asked.

"Consider marrying you. It's not impossible."

Henry let out a long breath. "That doesn't sound very flattering."

"It's not, not really. It's practical."

"I was hoping to be something a little more than *practical*," Henry complained.

"We've barely met. You can't expect there to be anything more."

"I liked *you* from the beginning."

Heat rose in Rose's cheeks. "Well . . . thank you. But that's the rose-tinted glasses of hindsight speaking."

"No, it's not," Henry insisted. "I did."

Rose glanced at the door, embarrassed to think of her sisters overhearing any of it.

Henry glanced at the door, too, and cleared his throat.

"So . . . the answer's maybe?" he said.

Rose nodded. "Maybe."

Henry rubbed his forehead. "Does that mean I should stop sabotaging myself with your father?"

"Did you think that was sabotage?" Rose asked with amusement. "No, by all means, keep going. He *loves* persuading people to do something they're reluctant to do."

Henry looked ill.

CHAPTER 9
Eavesdropping

As dinner wrapped up, Rose pushed away her half-eaten piece of cherry upside-down cake, which was soggy in the middle, and cleared her throat.

"Papa," she said. "May I have a word with you?"

Rose's father turned a deaf ear. "Henry, do you play cards?"

"Sometimes, when my roommates and I aren't too busy."

"Good lad. Come, play with me."

"Uh, don't you usually need four people?"

"We'll make do," Rose's father said. He thumped his arm around Henry's shoulders. "Do you know gin rummy?"

"No . . ."

"Papa!" Rose snapped. "We need to talk!"

"I don't see what we have to talk about," Rose's father growled, barely glancing at her.

Rose drew in a deep breath, trying not to lose her temper. "Remember? Last week, I told you that we needed to talk about my classes next semester. You said we'd talk about it next week. It's next week now, and I have my schedule planned out. The first class I need to take —"

"Just a small wager between friends, eh?" Rose's father said to Henry.

"*Wager?*"

41

"Papa!" Rose shouted.

"Come with me. I'll teach you the game." Rose's father shoved his chair back and pulled Henry up to his feet. Henry flicked a panicked look over at Rose, then a panicked look back at Rose's father, as the man dragged him down the hallway.

"The first class I need to take," Rose shouted, following after them, "is —"

The door to her father's study slammed in her face. There was a clicking sound.

Rose stared at the solid oak door, fuming. He always did this. It was maddening.

"You're never going to get through to him that way, dear," Rose's mother said, passing by and carrying two crumb-covered plates. "He doesn't like to lose arguments. He likes to win."

"Then how am I supposed to convince him?" Rose demanded.

Her sisters scampered over, each carrying an empty glass. They each pressed their glass to the door and their right ear to the end of the glass.

"Have you two no shame?" Rose asked.

"Shhhh!" Louise said, putting her finger to her lips. "Papa's explaining the rules now."

"He wants him to make a wager of five dollars," Sara said. "Mr. Wainscott made a choking sound."

"Now he's saying he doesn't have any money on him at all," Louise said. "I bet he's lying."

"No wonder, if Papa wants him to bet a month's worth of groceries," Rose snorted.

"Papa's saying Mr. Wainscott can owe him," Sara said. She was silent for a moment. "Mr. Wainscott refused."

"Now Papa's *really* keen," Louise said. "He's offering ten-to-one odds. And a handicap. He's really confident, isn't he?"

"Papa usually is," Rose said. She'd heard him bragging to her mother once that he could beat his friends more often if he wanted to, but it was better to make sure they kept on coming.

"Mr. Wainscott still refused. Now Papa's saying they can do a practice round first, and then twenty-to-one odds."

42

"He should really take Papa up on that," Sara opined.

"He did!" Louise cried. "He's saying he'll bet five cents!"

"He should've done more than that," Sara said. "Papa will probably let him win the first round."

"Five cents is still a lot of money," Rose said. "That's a trip on the subway."

"Shhhh!" Louise said, putting her finger to her lips. She listened for a long moment, intently.

Rose's mother walked by with two more crumb-covered plates.

"Do you want help clearing the table?" Rose asked her.

"No, no, dear," Rose's mother said. "Would you like a glass so you can listen with your sisters?"

"I am not a nosy busybody," Rose said huffily, "unlike some people, who —"

"They're talking about you, they're talking about you, they're talking about you!" Sara gasped. She yanked her ear away from the glass and gestured at Rose. "Come listen, come listen!"

Rose hesitated, but her younger sister grabbed her and shoved her ear against the glass.

There was a muffled, echoing quality, but she could hear the sounds surprisingly well. There was noise as her father expertly shuffled the deck, partly drowning out Henry's words.

"— to thank you for not letting her take science classes," Henry was saying. "That's not really a woman's place, is it?"

There was a scuffing sound as Rose's father dealt the cards. "Of course not. That would be ridiculous."

Rose's mouth gaped. *What in the world is he doing?*

"It doesn't matter that she's smarter than me," Henry said. "In fact, it would be embarrassing if people realized it."

"It's not so bad," Rose's father said. "Mabel's got a great head on her shoulders. She can balance a budget like no one else."

"But that's a useful skill," Henry said. "Not like paleontology."

Rose was mad as hornets. She envisioned the tongue-lashing she would give that liar at the first opportunity.

"Hear, hear!" Rose's father agreed. "What good does ancient history do anyone today, I ask you? Nothing!"

"Especially given the cost of college," Henry said. "It's just not worth it without the guarantee of a well-paying job afterwards!"

Ha! Rose thought, smirking. Hearing people say that was one of her father's pet peeves. It was his greatest regret that he'd never gone to college, even though he made plenty of money.

"Education does have value for its own sake," Rose's father said stiffly.

"But only when it's something useful," Henry said. "Not when it's something useless like geology or art history."

There was thunderous silence.

Rose bit her knuckle to keep from laughing. Her father had dozens of art history books in his study. How had Henry missed those?

"Besides, it's not like she would actually follow through and get all the degrees that would be necessary," Henry went on blithely.

"Watch your tongue," Rose's father growled. "Follow-through is not that girl's problem. Abominable stubbornness is."

"That's only if she wants to get the degrees," Henry said. "She doesn't really, you know."

What? Rose gaped indignantly.

"Then you don't know her at all," Rose's father snapped. "She hasn't shut up about it since she was nine years old. Wish I'd never bought her that book about dragons."

"That's just it. She didn't originally realize how much work it would be. Now she can't back down because her pride is at stake. Think about it: why hasn't she applied for a scholarship, if she's so stubborn and she wants to do it?"

Because I don't want to take the money away from students whose parents can't afford their tuition! Rose thought furiously. *My father can pay, so he should do it!*

"Hmmm," Rose's father said. There was a flipping sound. "I win."

"Do you want to play again?" Henry said. "I'll up the bet to ten cents."

Sara squeezed between Louise and Rose with a fresh glass in her hand. "What did I miss?"

44

Chapter 9: Eavesdropping

"He lost the first round, and now he's upping the bet," Louise informed her. "I don't think Papa likes him. He beat him in the first round."

"Ooh! If Papa doesn't care if he comes back, he'll squash him in every round. I wonder how long he'll last," Sara grinned, putting her glass against the door and pressing her ear to it.

"No, thank you," Rose's father said stiffly. There was a scraping sound, then several pounding footsteps. Rose dropped the glass and scrambled out of the way just in time.

Her sisters didn't. They tumbled into the room as the door swung open.

"Hello, nosy twits," Rose's father rumbled.

"Hello, Papa," the girls chorused innocently.

"Rose!" her father snapped, looking around. "There you are. Let's talk about those classes you want to take."

CHAPTER 10
Effrontery

P lease tell me that worked," Henry said, as Rose stepped out of her family's house, half an hour later, in something of a daze.

Rose spun around and shot him a glare. How dare he loiter around after her father had kicked him out of the house? Had he no sense or dignity?

"Hold on," Henry said, putting his hands in front of him. "I'm sure your sisters told you what I said —"

"They didn't have to," Rose said coldly. "I heard it myself."

Henry stared at her for a moment. "Eavesdropper!" he cried.

"Talking behind my back!" Rose shot back.

"All right, I was," Henry said, his mouth twitching. "But did it work?"

"Did what work?" Rose asked suspiciously.

"Did he agree to let you take the classes you want to take?" Henry asked, slowly and patiently.

Rose stared at him for a long moment. Her anger dissolved. "You did that on purpose?"

"Of course I did," Henry said. "I didn't mean any of that nonsense. Wasn't it obvious?"

"No, it wasn't," Rose said slowly. "But I suppose if it had been, it wouldn't have worked."

Chapter 10: Effrontery

"So it *did* work?" Henry asked, his eyes brightening.

Rose glanced back at the house nervously. She indicated with her head and started walking back in the direction of her apartment. She hoped her sisters hadn't been listening at the windows. Henry followed at a loping pace.

Once they were a safe distance away, Rose picked up the conversation again as they walked.

"He immediately started arguing with me about all the things you said. I kept protesting, because he kept trying to rebut arguments I'd never said or even believed, but that just made him more vehement. It was rather bizarre to have him insisting that I do something I've been begging him to let me do for ten years."

"So you're taking the classes you want to next semester?" Henry grinned.

"I hope so," Rose said, twirling her finger through a bracelet on her wrist. "He's insisting on helping me rearrange things . . . because apparently I can't possibly choose the ideal class schedule on my own . . . but I think that's just because he wants to feel useful." She glanced over at Henry as they kept on walking. "That was a rather brilliant idea."

"It was your idea," Henry shrugged. "You said he liked to talk people into things. I figured that meant it would be helpful to put him on your side, instead of against you. I was just hoping it wouldn't backfire horribly."

"You mean, like the effrontery at the museum?" Rose asked.

"Exactly."

"And like telling my family we were engaged when we weren't?"

Henry's face twisted. "Yes. Like that."

Rose smiled.

"In all seriousness," Henry said, looking over at her, "what *are* we going to do about the egg? We can't just leave him sitting there forever."

"I think," Rose said seriously, "we need to first arrange a place to bring him. Then we can worry about relocating him."

"I was thinking I'd take him home," Henry said.

"Do you have roommates?" Rose asked.

"Yes."

"Did you ask them how they'd feel about you bringing in a baby with a capacity to scream telepathically?"

Henry hesitated.

"I thought not," Rose said. "I doubt my roommates would be any more enthralled about the prospect."

Henry paused. "Marry me," he said.

Rose stared at him. "Excuse me?"

"Marry me," he repeated. "If you marry me, we can move in together, and we'll have a place to put him."

"That's not very romantic," Rose said.

"It's not romantic," Henry said, "it's practical. But I hope it could be more, in time."

"My father hates you, you know," Rose said. "You really *did* sabotage yourself this time. I doubt he'd give his permission."

Henry winced.

"But maybe," Rose said. She paused, and smiled. "Probably."

The next day was a quiet one. Rose and her roommates went to church in the morning, where Penelope sang off-key and Natalie made a big show of putting two dollars in the collection plate. Then, as soon as they got home, Natalie turned on the radio and Penelope pulled out stacks of homework, both seeming to forget their earlier piety.

Rose didn't tell them about Henry, or the dragon egg. How could she? It was still too new, too private. She stayed in her room for most of the day, thinking.

Monday afternoon, she met Henry outside of the Museum of Natural History fifteen minutes after lunchtime.

"Are we ready for this?" Henry asked. "They might kick us out again."

"If you feel a snide remark coming on, keep your mouth shut," Rose told him.

Chapter 10: Effrontery

"I wasn't trying to be rude before!" he protested.

"I remind you of a certain long string of epithets."

Henry hesitated. "Fair point."

"Have you spoken with your professors about using the empty laboratory?" Rose asked.

"I spoke to the dean. He gave me two weeks. I have the key." Henry pulled a long string out from under his shirt, with a key dangling from it. "I know it's not ideal for you, because City College is an hour and a half walk away . . ."

"You want to be a parent more than I do. It's only fair that you have closer access than me."

They stared up at the building.

"Of course, this is all predicated on whether or not we can get him out of there," Rose said. "It might take months before they're willing."

"And by then, we'd be married," Henry said.

Rose bit her lip. She'd given him a tentative *yes* this morning, but her stomach still clenched whenever she thought about it. She hoped she'd be more willing to consider setting a date soon, because two weeks wasn't long. They should probably be looking for an apartment already.

Henry took her hand. She looked down. Then she nodded, and they walked up the stairs to the museum.

Nobody stopped them from entering the doors, so they headed straight for the stairs. They were nearly on the third floor when they spotted Director Campbell on his way down.

"Oh, no," Henry moaned. "Here we go again . . ."

"You!" the director shouted, pointing at Henry. His eyes were bloodshot and wild. "Get upstairs! Get upstairs right now!"

"What?" Henry looked dumbfounded. "I thought you were going to kick me out."

"Do you know how long it's been since I've slept?!" the director shouted. "*Thirty-six hours!* It's asking for you. It's screaming for you. It won't *stop* screaming for you. Make it stop!"

Henry didn't need to be told twice. He raced up the stairs, two at a time.

Rose hesitated. "Are you all right, Director Campbell?" she asked. There were circles under his eyes that were dark enough to use as inkwells.

"That thing has to get out of my museum," the director said wildly. "No one can go up to the fourth floor. I keep trying to calm it down. It won't calm down! It needs to leave!"

"Can I get that in writing, sir?" Rose asked tentatively.

The director fumbled through his pockets, yanked out a notebook and pen from an inner pocket, and scribbled something down. He ripped off the piece of paper and handed it to her. *Director Campbell authorizes taking the living dragon egg out of the museum,* it said, with a signature at the bottom.

Rose sighed with relief. It wasn't everything they would need — it wasn't even permanent custody — but it was enough to start with.

"Thank you, sir," she said politely, nodding her head.

Then ran up the rest of the stairs to help her fiancé with the screaming baby.

CHAPTER 11
Everything

You know, I never really thought I'd be looking forward to the day my first child hatched," Henry said, running his hands over the leathery surface of the egg. According to Mr. Teedle, it felt softer to touch now than it used to. The other eggs were all hard and slick. Rose couldn't compare herself because she hadn't been allowed to touch them.

"It was your idea," Rose said, paging through her textbook. She was doing her homework here because it was a better use of time than sitting around doing nothing, and the egg didn't care what she did, as long as she was here as long as possible. "Don't complain."

"Oh, I'm not complaining," Henry said. "It's just . . . sometimes it's still surprising. You know?"

"I know," Rose said. She wrote down a note in the margin of her textbook, and turned the page.

"I want to give him everything," Henry said longingly. "I want to give him the world."

"You don't own the world," Rose said tartly. "But there is something that we probably ought to give him."

Henry sat up straighter. "What?" he asked.

"A name. We can't keep calling him 'the dragon' or 'the baby' forever."

"Good point," Henry said. "We do know the gender already."

Rose shut her textbook. "What do you say, dragon?" she asked. "Shall we give you a name?"

A name! He didn't know what a name was. Was it something to eat? He looked forward to learning to eat. Crunch crunch!

"What kind of name would suit him?" Henry asked thoughtfully.

"I suppose we could go with something descriptive," Rose said. "Spiny or Spiky or . . . no."

"No," Henry said.

"No. That sounds too much like a pet's name."

"A human name, then," Henry said. "Are there any you like?"

"James. Or John. Or William. How about you?"

"Commodore, Virgil, and Bartholomew," Henry said promptly.

Rose stared at him. "You have strange taste in names."

"The girl names I like are Louvenia, Glendora, and Pleasant," Henry added.

"I can't tell whether you're serious or joking."

"Oh, I'm perfectly serious."

Rose wrinkled her nose.

"How about we use one of your names, and one of mine?" Henry asked.

"Virgil's not bad," Rose said. "That could be a first name. How about for a middle name?"

"I guess the least boring one is . . . James?"

"All right," Rose said. "Virgil James . . ."

". . . Wainscott," Henry added.

Rose shivered. Somehow, adding in the last name made it seem real.

"What do you think?" Henry asked the egg, running his hands along its orange-and-brown surface. "Are you Virgil James?"

He was something. He was happy. He was hungry. No, he wasn't hungry. He didn't know how to be hungry. He was going to wiggle his toes.

There was a knock on the door to the laboratory. Rose got up to answer it.

Chapter 11: Everything

Mr. Teedle stood there, his face pale. He held a rolled-up newspaper in his hands.

"Have you two seen this?" he asked in a shaking voice.

"Has news gotten out about Virgil already?" Rose asked, alarmed.

"Virgil?" Mr. Teedle looked confused.

"We named the dragon," Henry said.

"Oh. No, news has not gotten out about this dragon egg. The museum's still not planning to release a press statement until he's been hatched. But look."

Mr. Teedle unrolled the newspaper and thumped it on the table. On the front page, in bold letters, it declared, *DRAGON EGG HATCHES AT MUSEUM!*

Rose stared at the paper blankly. There was a picture of a *Deinonychus antirrhopus* dragon egg with a tiny snout just starting to protrude from the top. She glanced at the caption underneath the picture. "The Dragon National Monument?" she said slowly.

"Where the eggs were found," Mr. Teedle said, breathing heavily. "They have sixty of them on display. A vacationing couple passed by one of them, and . . . *crack!*"

Virgil liked that noise. He repeated it. Crack! Crack!

Rose stared at the picture. She stared at the egg. She stared at Henry.

"Then that means," she said slowly, "that it's not just *one* dragon egg that's alive . . ."

Mr. Teedle nodded. *"All* of them are."

58307690R00039

Made in the USA
San Bernardino, CA
26 November 2017